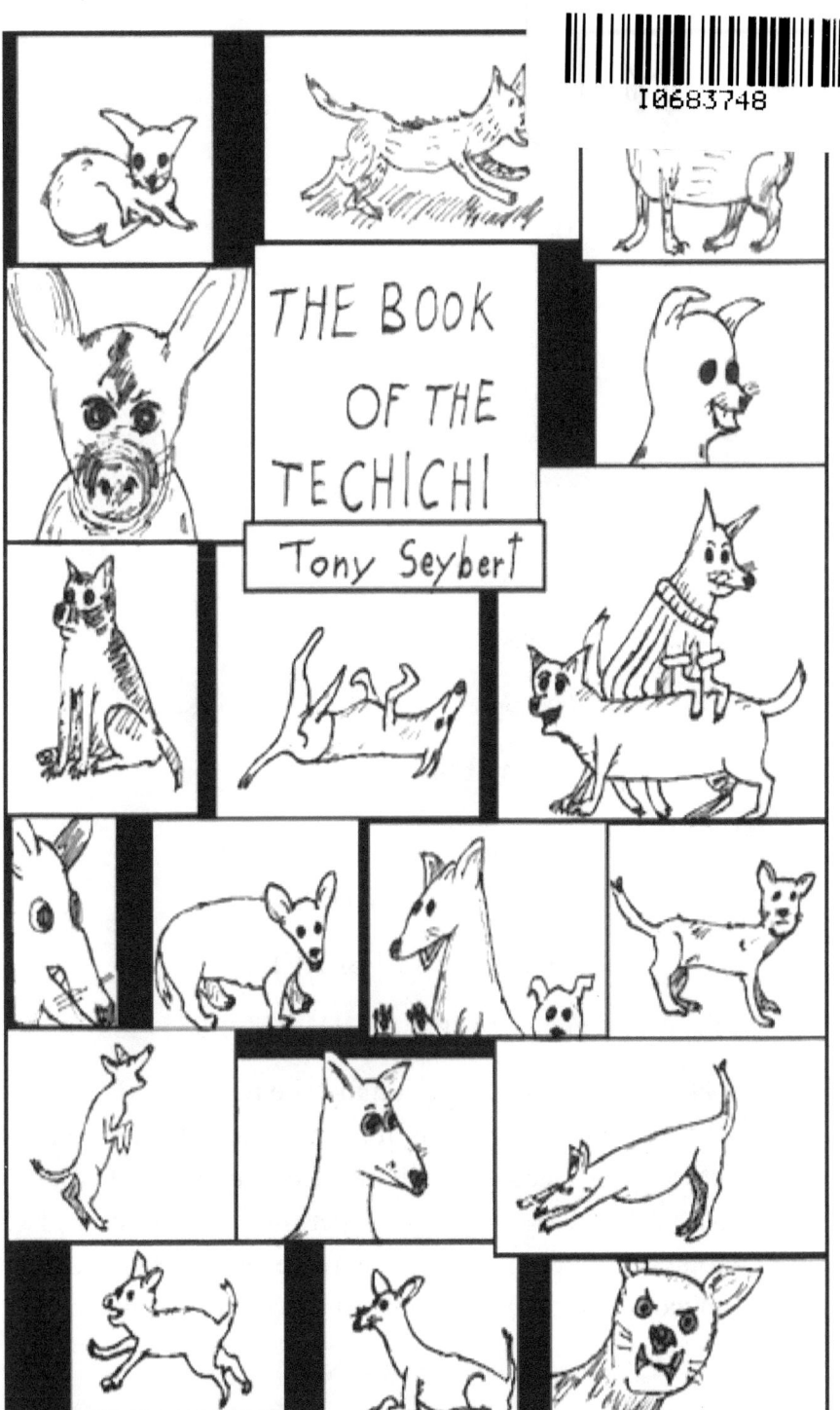

THE BOOK

OF THE

TECHICHI

Tony Seybert

AFFLATUS PRESS PUBLISHING

Thousand Oaks, CA 91359

The Book of the Techichi

by Tony Seybert

TABLE OF CONTENTS

INTRODUCTION

"The Chihuahua dog, which as late as 25 years ago was quite commonly to be found in Mexico, is a curious little creature, popularly supposed to be a cross breed between the prairie dog and a jackrabbit. The animal resembles a small dog, whose weight is sometimes not over one and a half pounds, with a disproportionately large head, bulging eyes and long ears. The hair is usually scanty, showing the pink skin underneath. One of the marks is said to be an unclosed cranial fissure, through which the brain can be felt throbbing underneath the skin. These little animals are particularly destructive and are constantly scratching at things with their long claws. They are quite susceptible of taming, if taken young, and in numerous instances, the breed has been domesticated, although they seldom show the usual dog traits of sagacious and intelligent attachment."

-Consul General A.L.M. Gottschalk of Mexico City, quoted in the Stockton Independent, September 8, 1908

I woke up this morning with Koti in my armpit. He's a toy Chihuahua, weighing about four pounds and he's twelve years old. Koti is just about the best friend I've ever had.

(Eliza the cat is also just about the best friend I've ever had, but it's not always about you, Eliza!)

Koti is blind in one eye, and his tongue sticks out of his mouth, mostly on the left side because he has no teeth. His whole jaw sags because he is missing part of his jawbone.

My nickname for Koti is the Mojave Mole Rat.

He is beautiful.

Koti is magic.

Sometimes, he runs in and whimpers and scampers around in a circle in front of me to get my attention. I follow him to the backyard (he goes through the dog door) and he runs around in a figure-eight.

He's so excited!

Not about anything in particular.

"It's the world! Look at the world, Tony! Isn't it wonderful! I wanted us to see it together!"

I don't know how else to translate.

I really love the little guy.

He's not the only Chihuahua in the house. We have six dogs, and they are all Chihuahuas or Chihuahua mixes.

Lulu is the oldest. She's nearly 20 years old. She likes to sit in the sun. She has no interest in imparting her wisdom to the others. She's earned her rest. Every once in a while, she hops up on a kitchen chair to steal a piece of steak off the plate of an unwary diner. Just to remind us that she's still in the game, I think.

Gin-Gin is about ten. She's just about the sweetest dog I've ever seen. She grunts at you and then rolls over on her back so you can scratch her tummy! She's so happy! She's a little overweight. She looks like an eggplant with a little doggy head. I doubt that she weighs more than eight pounds.

Gin-Gin is the only one of the dogs that likes Koti. He is a brat.

He walks over the reclining bodies of the other dogs to get across the couch. He's the only boy dog, and he thinks very highly of himself. He's my best friend, but I must admit that he's kind of an ass. You know how it is.

Gin-Gin's best buddy is Shiva, the biggest of the dogs. Shiva is part Chihuahua, part terrier (I guess) and part … something else. She's twice as big as any of the others, maybe even approaching thirty pounds. Shiva never throws her weight around … except when she feels the youngsters are fighting too much or harassing the senior dogs.

Gin-Gin and Shiva are almost inseparable. Constant companions. They are always cuddling together on the back of the couch. And they always investigate the yard together when it's time to go outside.

The young ones are Chiquis and Pachi. Chiquis is about three years old and Pachi is 15 months. We got Pachi as a buddy for Chiquis so she wouldn't harass the senior dogs so relentlessly. This plan has been somewhat successful.

Chiquis and Pachi attack each other nonstop all day, growling and playing and fighting. But sometimes they get bored with that. And they start giving the senior dogs a hard time. They are a couple of juvenile delinquents, a Chihuahua street gang, stubbornly hostile to an older generation that just doesn't understand. I think of The Wild One, the Marlon Brando film about the motorcycle ruffians.

"What are you rebelling against, Pachi?"

"What do ya got?" Pachi responds.

"I done see a Chihuahua dog on de bleachers, and dat dog am a powerful hoodoo."

- San Diego Union and Daily Bee, June 28, 1899

They are beautiful and magical creatures. Is it strange that any

Chihuahua devotee would decide to transfer some of that feeling of wonder to a story or a whole book? Some years ago, I started getting ideas for stories about Chihuahuas, and I started making notes and writing them down, and eventually I had enough for a book.

The Chihuahua dog is named after a province in northern Mexico. Perhaps this large desert area is where it was first bred. Perhaps not. The history of the Chihuahua dog is a bit mysterious, but there are enough clues to put together a historical narrative that is probably mostly true, in a general sense.

Small dogs have been a part of the story of the Americas for thousands of years. When the Spanish conquistadors terrorized and conquered Mexico in the 1500s, the inhabitants of southern Mexico had long co-existed with a species of small dog called the Techichi. These dogs are believed to have been domesticated by the Toltecs several hundred years before they were conquered by the Aztecs. The Techichi were bred for companionship and hunting, and they were also used for food. The Aztecs bred them to be smaller than the Toltec version of the Techichi.

Pottery and temple art in many places across Central America depict dogs that look like Chihuahuas in many respects.

Is the Techichi the same as the Chihuahua? This seems unlikely. DNA testing by the KTH Royal Institute of Technology in Stockholm indicates that the modern Chihuahua shares up to 70% of its DNA with ancient dog breeds of the Americas. So they are not exactly the same.

Spanish records show that the Techichi did not thrive under colonial rule. They were eaten by the thousands and may have been nearly wiped out.

They must have survived in isolated places here and

there. And interbred with some of the dogs brought over by Europeans.

By the mid-1800s, American tourists returned from Mexico with tales of small dogs and how precious they were. These small dogs were referred to as "Texas dogs," "Arizona dogs" or "Mexico dogs." But by the 1880s, they were most commonly known as Chihuahua dogs.

"The smallest dog is probably the Chihuahua of Mexico. It can snuggle in the palm of your hand or may be concealed in a bunch of flowers."

- Mill Valley Independent, December 3, 1909

The popularity of the faithful Chihuahua has waxed and waned in the many decades since he was identified as a Texas dog or an Arizona dog. These little canine treasures gained a mark of much-earned credibility in 1904 when the American Kennel Club registered its first Chihuahua, a little fellow named Midget, owned by H. Raynor of Texas.

Interest in the little dogs was rekindled in 1916 to 1917 when members of the National Guard returned from Mexico, where they had been chasing Pancho Villa for 11 months. Many of them brought Chihuahuas with them into the U.S., and as the reputation of these quirky little canine companions spread through the nation, demand skyrocketed. A 1917 story from the Associated Press says that "small boys are searching all of the homes of refugees from the interior of the state for these diminutive little animals."

A more recent wave of popularity for our yappy little friends began in the 1990s with Taco Bell's "Yo quiero Taco Bell" campaign and its taco-hungry Chihuahua named Gidget. They are still very popular and it's easy to see why. They may be yappy and jealous and at times a little demented, but they are loyal and friendly and full of personality.

"Every Mexican owns at least one Chihuahua Chiquita dog. They are beautiful little creatures, and of two varieties – one with long, silky hair; the other with a short, smooth coat that is as soft as velvet to the touch. I have seen full-grown specimens that weighed a trifle over a pound, and young puppies about the size of field mice. They have large expressive eyes and the best of dispositions."

- Santa Cruz Sentinel, February 27, 1886

My first Chihuahua was a senior, deer-headed dog named Angelica, and she changed my life for the short time I had her.

I never had any trouble getting up early to make sure she got her morning walk before I went to work.

She liked riding around in the car and sleeping on the passenger seat. She got along with cats and most dogs, but she really hated white or tan dogs that weighed more than 35 pounds! They were bad! And I couldn't convince her otherwise. One time I was taking her for a walk and Angelica chased away a coyote that stepped into the road about ten feet away from us! She charged the offending animal, barking at full volume, and the coyote looked a little embarrassed and pivoted back into the brush.

Angelica is no longer with us. She was a senior dog when I got her, and I knew she wouldn't be around forever, but I had hoped it would be longer than the fifteen months we had together. You could tell she was old from the white specks on her muzzle and her missing teeth. But she didn't act old! Angelica saw a chain-link fence and saw a ladder, and she would soon be looking at you from the other side if you didn't keep an eye on her. She wouldn't run away. She would wait for you. Getting out of enclosures was a game to her.

I was lucky to have her love and friendship for

those months, and I'm lucky to have Chihuahuas still in my life. I hope I'm always so lucky that I'm always able to live and thrive with Chihuahuas and their magic!

THE LOST VERSES OF THE SONG OF MOSES

1 And God the Tetragrammaton, with trembling lips that smelt of beets, said unto me that he could see that the children of Israel would soon forget the covenant. For the covenant is long and hard to remember.

2 Plus, let us face it, it is rather arbitrary and random, and penalizes many things that are pleasing to the children of Israel.

3 So they will turn to other gods! And this pleaseth not God the Tetragrammaton.

4 And God the Tetragrammaton told me, I mean, said unto me that when the children of Israel fall into evil ways and go to the brothels and slide into vegetarianism and look too much at tentacle porn.

5 And gaze upon naked people in French and Italian art and partake too freely of glory holes and listen to RAP (which they ought to call CRAP) and gaze too long at girls in sailor suits and make rude remarks about Jason Momoa's chest.

6 And read comic books and many other things not approved by the covenant – like getting a tattoo or lacking intact testicles – then shall God the Tetragrammaton plague the children of Israel with the Chihuayim.

7 Yea, the Chihuayim, the little yappy dogs. The Chihuayim, they shalt be a plague on the children of Israel when they become loose in their ways.

8 For the Chihuayim will bark and bark at everyone who walks past on the sidewalk. And the Chihuayim will puke on the folded blanket on the couch right after you have washed it.

9 And the Chihuayim shalt eat bottle caps, and the vet shalt charge you many talents to remove these. And the Chihuayim will have bad teeth and a bad smell from his mouth and you will have to brush his teeth and it will be an ordeal.

10 And the Chihuayim will poop on the floor in shadow and you will not see. And the Chihuayim will pee on your socks, not knowing the difference between your socks and the pee pad.

11 All these things and more shall be the duty of the Chihuayim. They shall be a blight on the land.

12 And the children of Israel shall be blind to this plague, and shall keep them and feed them and pay their vet bills and neglect the harvest to make sure they get their walkies.

13 This God the Tetragrammaton shall do to the unsuspecting children of Israel when they shall break the covenant.

THUS ENDETH THE LOST VERSES OF THE SONG OF MOSES

THE BOOK OF ZEKAH, the HOLY CHIHUAHUA

Chapter 1

1 Mary and Joseph the Holy Parents didst enjoy a quiet evening at home in Nazareth when their Chihuahua, whose name was Zekah, did commence barking and yapping.

2 "It is the Messenger of the Lord," Joseph didst say unto Zekah. "The Angel means no harm. So shut it, you daft beastie."

3 But it was to no avail and Zekah didst bark and the Angel of the Lord could not make himself heard and finally he did cast upon the beast a peanut butter treat and Zekah did take herself to her bed to eat the treat.

4 And finally the Angel of the Lord did make clear to Joseph that he should take his wife and flee because King Herod had ordered the death of all firstborn children because of a dream he had after eating fried Polish sausage with onions, peppers and beer mustard.

5 "That would do it," Joseph did say to the Angel of the Lord. "I suppose it would," replied the Angel. "I'm not real eager to test it." And they both laughed, again arousing Zekah's suspicions that the Angel was not really a good sort.

Chapter 2

1 So Joseph did heed the words of the Angel of the Lord and he did take his wife Mary and didst load her onto a donkey along with a few suitcases.

2 And also, at Mary's insistence, they took Zekah the Chihuahua with them because Mary did not trust her in-laws to tend to Zekah, nor did she trust her own family. Nay, neither did she trust the Cohens next door or the Spencers across the street.

3 "For Zekah," Mary said, "has a sensitive stomach and needs a special diet. And she needs to get her walkies."

4 "Also, I fear they will not brush her teeth, and it is important to brush a little dog's teeth."

5 And Joseph did acquiesce, saying, "OK OK Sheesh."

6 And Joseph and Mary didst make their way to the town of Bethlehem to the inn where the innkeeper's wife had naturally curly hair.

7 Joseph was signing the register when Zekah didst commence her yapping when skateboarders went by.

8 And the innkeeper didst refuse to give Joseph and Mary a room because they didn't allow dogs. Mary said she preferred sleeping in the manger anyway so Hmmph.

Chapter 3

1 During the night, the shepherds gathered on a hill with their lunchboxes and some beer. They heard a sound in the night.

2 "Do you hear what I hear?" said the first shepherd. "A sound! A sound!"

3 "Yeah, I heard it," said the second shepherd. "It's probably Mary and Joseph's dog. She always makes a racket when the Angel of the Lord flies by. I figure the Angel of the Lord will be along in a minute to tell us of some news of the utmost importance."

4 And sure enough, the Angel of the Lord did soon appear to them. "You look like you were expecting me," he did say, making conversation.

5 "Yeah, we heard all that yapping," said the shepherds.

6 And the Angel of the Lord did say to them, "Yeah, Mary and Joseph's fucking dog. It barks at everything. Camels, ants, soldiers of pharaoh, cherubim, seraphim, aluminum. Nothing gets past that dog. Anyway, I bring you tidings of great joy for unto Mary is born Christ the Savior."

7 And the shepherds be like, "Cool, man."

Chapter 4

1 And soon the child was born unto Mary. And they had just got the Holy Child to sleep when Zekah started barking like a crazy dog. "O what is it now?" said Joseph. "A cockroach, a mouse, a bedbug?"

2 But lo and behold, it was three wise men from the East, Gaspar, Balthazar and the other one, following the star to Bethlehem. They tried to explain their mission to Joseph but it was difficult with Zekah running around and jumping on their legs and barking and growling.

3 But finally Mary picked Zekah up and calmed her and the Wise Men were able to explain they had come with gifts to honor the Holy Child who was the Light and Hope of the World.

4 "That sounds like a lot to expect of a little baby," said Joseph, but the Wise Men did not hear and Mary said to them that she was calling the child Jesus after her favorite blues singer.

5 And Mary did put Zekah down to greet the Wise Men, and Zekah did soon pee on the frankincense and then she ate the myrrh and vomited it back up and thus did Joseph put the gold in a safe place.

6 The Wise Men soon left to continue their pilgrimage to honor the other miraculous children born to virgins.

7 Jesus, Mary and Joseph soon returned to Nazareth where Zekah resumed her position as Lord of the House.

THE GIANTS

O Ye Most Blessed and Silly Techichi, the Glorious and Gracious Offspring of Ouaca the Terrible and Benevolent, within whose scanty fur nestle all the virtues, hiding among the lice and fleas and ticks.

Gather ye round, O Children of the Great Hound …

Know ye, O Children of the Giants in Their Own Minds …

That there was a time long after the Great Beginning when the Techichi roamed Aztlan from the isthmus to the Mojave …

They called themselves the Giants, though they seldom exceeded ten pounds, but they thought themselves the biggest and grandest and greatest and bravest of the many folk of Aztlan, and they were giants in their own minds and giants in their own hearts.

But they knew there had once been a time, not so very long ago, perhaps, when the Techichi had been as big as their hearts! And as big as their spirits! And they had ruled the land of Aztlan, yea, and far beyond Aztlan, from the land where your pee freezes in the air, across the mountains and the deserts and the marshes and the rivers and the plains and the valleys and the volcanoes, all the way to Land's End, far to the South, where they say the land is on fire and the great waves crash against the cliffs, where there live the strange people with their faces on their bellies!

Or so it is said.

As a matter of fact, the Giants were so big that it was a bit of a problem.

The Techichi were always knocking each other off cliffs and bridges and sidewalks and getting stuck in doors.

It was often difficult for them to find enough to eat as it took three or four brontosauruses for them to feel full.

It was bad for the environment too. They flattened trees and destroyed ecosystems and caused the topsoil to fall into the sea.

The great gods, high in their cloud city of Mu-Dule-Zik -Zok, were unconcerned and mostly unaware of the problem. They had great god concerns and didn't much bother about things in Aztlan.

Until one day, three Techichi were wandering around Mu-Dule-Zik-Zok, crushing the statues, trampling the foliage, knocking lesser gods over the railings and interrupting the po-lo games.

I say," said Du-Zok, the god of bees and potty secrets. "What is going on?"

"Heavens! Don't ask me," exclaimed Nok-Unu-Deen, the goddess of coffee and liniment, who is known by the sign of the elbow kiss. "It seems to be some of those mortal crea-tures from the lands below."

"And they're bigger than shit!" said Flik-Ik, the god of nursery rhymes, a little more restrained than usual.

"Wait! Somebody expel them!" ordered Kev-M-Mikta, the goddess of bird hats and chewing gum. "They have disturbed my tea time and upset my guests!"

It wasn't much trouble to awaken one of the Ezad-dun, the giant servants of the great gods. They sleep for millennia, waiting to be called to service.

Although the Techichi were big, they weren't as big as an Ezad. Kev-M-Mikta called out: "Don't hurt them! They are too cute!" So the Ezad chased them around, picked them up and put them gently back down on the trembling ground in Aztlan.

They bit his fingers and wrists several times, but the Ezad remained impassive, except for a slight increase in his face's frowniness.

"It's your own fault," said Kev-M-Mikta to the Ezad. "You have to talk to them and get their trust."

The Ezad rolled his eyes and went back to his cave to hibernate until called to service again.

"Well," said Du-Zok. "How did that happen?"

The great gods quickly lost interest in HOW it happened. They just wanted to make sure it didn't happen again.

What had happened was this:

Wowwow and two of his friends among the Techichi were frolicking loudly in the mountains when they saw the cloud city.

Wowwow was the first in a long line of unruly Techichi with that name, who would be famous in their own minds in every generation. He was full of fun and inquisitiveness and quick to bark at intruders and just as quick to stop if distracted by a bug or a leaf or a hallucination.

"Hey! What's that?" he said, approaching the edge of the cloud city of the great gods and sniffing it.

The great gods thought that the cloud city was more than high enough to be out of reach of any mortal creature. But the Techichi were Giants! They were ginormous! It actually wasn't that hard for them to jump into the cloud city from the highest peak in Aztlan. And soon they were cavorting and carousing and wreaking havoc among the great gods.

So that was what happened.

The great gods convened a tribunal to discuss the issue of the Techichi and their silly bigness and their inclination towards disaster.

Kev-M-Mikta was chosen to serve as chairman. She feared for her collection of bird hats if there were further incursions.

Du-Zok had shown up to support his ally Kev-M-Mikta, but he really wasn't that interested and spent most of the time sleeping in his chair and sucking honey out of his own body through his belly button. (Actually, the honey came out of a special nipple just above his asshole. But this is frequently edited a bit for various reasons.)

Gziz-zin-tin-zugat, the goddess of cinnamon and muddy carpets that smell of insect death, also showed up to be on the committee. Poor Gziz-zin-tin-zugat! Marginalized by the great gods since the days of the War with the Apple-Faced Titans, she was happy to participate in this task that so few were interested in.

And that was all. Just these three. The great gods went back to their banqueting and their billiards and their golf.

Except Hochupinzakel.

Hochupinzakel, the Creator of Stars, manifested himself as a ladybug and buzzed around, whispering in the ears of these few gods who had shown up.

The Creator of Stars wanted something to be done! For Aztlan was his own particular creation, one of many creations, and he did not like to see it spoiled and dirtied by these Techichi who had become too big and too numerous.

"They have eaten all my lovely multi-colored monkeys!" he complained to Kev-M-Mikta.

"These Techichi are changing the shape of my carefully crafted continents!" whined Hochupinzakel to Du-Zok, who nodded carelessly but didn't stop sucking honey from his own belly button.

"And the poop! There is so much poop!" said the Creator of Stars to Gziz-zin-tin-zugat, who nodded sympathetically. "They are befouling the lakes and streams! Even ocean life is in danger!"

The tribunal adjourned for a few weeks or months to think about it.

And Wowwow and his minions visited Mu-Dule-Zik-Zok again, in much greater numbers this time.

You see, after Wowwow and his friends had been removed by the Ezad and placed back in the mortal realm, the other Techichi asked what had happened to them.

"We found the secret city of the great gods!" said Wowwow. "Mu-Dule-Zik-Zok! It's up in the mountains! It was so great!"

"It smells like rosemary!" said Uliga, one of Wowwow's companions.

"And like coffee grounds you dig out of the trash for some reason!" said Chiggers, Wowwow's best friend.

"And like a combination of dead chipmunk and horse poop and you want to roll in it!" added Wowwow.

And the Techichi got so excited by all this talk of the

wondrous smells of Mu-Dule-Zik-Zok that they made Wow-wow their King for All Time and persuaded him to lead them to this amazing place!

This time it was eighty or ninety Techichi frolicking and cavorting in the city of the great gods. The Techichi with their big hearts and their great spirits and their curiosity and their hyperactive inclinations and their destructive instincts and their pooping and their barfing and all that.

And don't forget! They were ginormous!

They wrecked Mu-Dule-Zik-Zok. The rampaging gigantic Techichi trashed the place. The palaces and the gardens and the amphitheaters and the nickelodeons and the soccer stadium and the aquarium and the heliport and the puppet show, all now rubble amidst the piles of poo and barf, the latter of which was mostly grass and rare houseplants.

The great gods again called upon the Ezad-dun, but the Ezad-dun are not numberless, and it took some time for them to gather up the Techichi and put them back in Aztlan from whence they had come.

And then the Ezad-dun had to clean up the rubble and the poop and the barf, and then they sprayed off all the urine that had dried on the walls and the fountains and the statuary and the murals and the tapestries.

And the Ezad-dun sterilized themselves by going to the sun for the weekend.

Oh wow! Did Du-Zok, Kev-M-Mikta and Gziz-zin-tin-zugat hear about it!

"What were you doing all these weeks and months!?"

"How could you let that happen again!?"

"You are stupid!"

"You better do something about it this time!"

"WHERE IS JUSTICE!?"

Not to mention the ire of Hochupinzakel, the Creator of Stars, who buzzed his vexation in their ears until they could not hear themselves except by shouting.

The tribunal conferred in private for a few minutes. They didn't want to admit that they hadn't done anything.

"They'll kill us or something," said Gziz-zin-tin-zugat.

"They won't kill us," said Du-Zok. "They will skin us and make curtains and rugs from our hides."

"And they will use our muscles to stuff cushions," said Kev-M-Mikta. "And our bones will be arranged into bookcases or telephone towers or cash registers or something of that nature."

"I hope somebody comes up with a good idea soon!' said Du-Zok, looking nervously at the crowd.

After the tribunal dithered for a few minutes and came up with a few ideas that ranged from horrifying to lethal, Gziz-zin-tin-zugat had a thought.

"Oh!" said Gziz-zin-tin-zugat. "I know! Let's call the Great Hound of the Cosmos!"

Du-Zok said, "What can he do?"

"Don't you see?" said Kev-M-Mikta. "It's brilliant. It doesn't matter if he fixes it or not. It moves the focus to him and away from us."

Du-Zok nodded. "Yes. Yes, I see. And it makes sense, doesn't it?

"The Techichi are the responsibility of the Great Hound of the Cosmos!"

(Which wasn't really true, but whatever, Du-Zok.)

The tribunal surreptitiously called for Whoot-Hoot-Woot, the god of whistling and ornate thimbles, and asked him to call for the Great Hound of the Cosmos.

So Whoot-Hoot-Woot went to the highest peak on Mu-

Dule-Zik-Zok and whistled for the Great Hound of the Cosmos.

The Great Hound of the Cosmos was far away, at the edge of the galaxy, peeing on one of the Ten Great Green Planets of the Farthest Star. The Great Hound was meticulous about marking his territory.

He heard the whistle of Whoot-Hoot-Woot with his ears perked up and his mouth smiling at a call he recognized.

"Why, it's Whoot-Hoot-Woot!" said the Great Hound. "I wonder what he wants! He is a good fellow. I shall attend to him by and by."

And so the Great Hound of the Cosmos trotted off in the general direction of Mu-Dule-Zik-Zok. He chased a comet circling the Great Red Sun of Rao. He veered off to eat something bright and orange and gross rotting on the surface of Ya-kin-12. The Great Hound of the Cosmos chased some Celestial Rabbits around and around the breath-taking pink spiral clusters of the Ninny Nebula.

While the Great Hound loped through the heavens on a circuitous course to Mu-Dule-Zik-Zok, the tribunal made a statement to the great gods who had gathered to find out what was to be done about the Techichi.

Kev-M-Mikta cleared her throat and read the statement. "We of the Techichi tribunal of Mu-Dule-Zik-Zok, after much time periods of discernment and care, have discussed several ideas about the further deportment of the problem of the Techichi! However! We realize that we might benefit from the sagacious input of the true patron of the Techichi. Thus, we have sent for the Great Hound of the Cosmos to come and consult with us in this vital matter!"

The great gods welcomed this announcement as a true sign of the wisdom of the great gods and, after much self-

praise and back-patting, everybody went home and started to clean up after the last destructive frolic of the Techichi.

And so, the Great Hound of the Cosmos thundered into Mu-Dule-Zik-Zok and greeted his friend Whoot-Hoot-Woot with much face-licking and tail-wagging and head-scratching.

Whoot-Hoot-Woot hesitated to tell the Great Hound why he had called him. The whistling god swallowed his embarrassment and told the Great Hound about the Techichi and the destruction of Mu-Dule-Zik-Zok.

The Great Hound of the Cosmos looked around and began to stomp and tromp around in the rubble.

"I like it like this!" he said. "It's a great improvement! Did you call me here to thank me? That wasn't necessary! The Techichi did it! I'm very proud of them, but I had nothing to do with it! You can thank them in person!

They'd like that."

"Uh, no," said Whoot-Hoot-Woot. "That's not it." He explained that the great gods considered it a bad thing and they didn't want it to happen again.

"So, I guess I'll take you over to see Kev-M-Mikta and she can convene the tribunal and then we can ..."

The Great Hound of the Cosmos interrupted him. "I love Kev-M-Mikta as I love all the beings of the Cosmos," said the Great Hound. "And I surely would love to see her and this tribunal. But I think I see the problem ... and I think I'd rather go to Aztlan and be among the Techichi and feel their great hearts and their great spirits and perhaps come up with a solution pleasing to all. Without any time spent on tribunals or committees. Could you give me an hour's head start before you tell them anything?"

Whoot-Hoot-Woot agreed and the Great Hound of the Cosmos charged off towards Aztlan to find the Techichi.

The Techichi rampaged across the land, so large and so active and so hungry. The Great Hound of the Cosmos found them quite easily and watched them for a few minutes.

How he admired their energy! And their boldness! And their unquenchable vigor for existence! Their playful-ness! Their quirks! Their bravery and their loyalty!

And of course, their great spirits and their great hearts.

And yet, as he smiled and his great cosmic heart filled with joy and love at sight of them, he saw room for improve-ment. They had undoubtedly improved Mu-Dule-Zik-Zok. But the Techichi had ruined Aztlan. Once a great green para-dise of fields and forests, Aztlan showed growing regions of desertification and despoliation, destruction and ruin. If their bodies remained as big as their hearts and their spirits, Aztlan would soon be worn away to dust and mud, and the oceans would eventually swallow it whole.

The Great Hound of the Cosmos looked around. "I'd better take care of this before Hochupinzakel finds me. I'll get an earful! I'm surprised he isn't here already!"

The Great Hound remembered the Techichi and their gracious and hospitable ways. They were big-hearted and proud and always helpful. They were giants in their own minds. Perhaps that was all that was necessary for them to remain the Techichi.

He leapt from the clouds to greet them.

"The Great Hound!" they cried. For he was their friend and protector. Wowwow and his tribe pranced over to meet him.

"The Great Hound! The Great Hound!"

After he had accepted their greetings, he ran with them, and chased the mice and rabbits with them, and rolled in foul-smelling piles.

And then, slyly, with all the tact of a celestial dog-being, the Great Hound subtly introduced the subject of his visit. "Aztlan is kind of a mess."

To which Wowwow replied, "Is it? We like it this way."

"Well, it's getting kind of worn out," replied the Great Hound of the Cosmos. "The poo is everywhere. The trees are nearly gone in places. The mountains are being ground down. And your great size … you're frightening the other animals."

"Yes, it's true," said Wowwow. "But what can we do? We are the Techichi! We are great of heart and great of spirit! Is there any other way for us to be in the world?"

The Great Hound considered. "Well, great Wowow, the Techichi are great of heart and great of spirit. But the Techichi also believe in fair play!"

Wowwow led the Techichi in a cheer of agreement. "Yes! The Techichi believe in fairness! And sportsmanship! And looking out for the little guy!"

"Well," said the Great Hound of the Cosmos. "Perhaps it would be more fair to the other animals if you had not quite so many gifts!"

Wowwow considered this. "Well, I don't know. We are great because of our big hearts! We must retain our big hearts!"

"Of course!" said the Great Hound.

"And our mighty spirits! We must keep our mighty spirits!"

"Oh, of course!" said the Great Hound of the Cosmos. "You wouldn't be the Techichi without your mighty spirits!"

"And our bravery!" added Wowwow. "And our great beauty! And our fierceness! And our great sense of humor! We are hilarious!"

"Yes, you are!" agreed the Great Hound. "None of these attributes shall be changed! For then you would not be the Techichi! Is there anything else you MUST have to be the Techichi?"

Wowwow considered the question. "I don't think so, Great Hound of the Cosmos!"

"Then I have what I need to know to bless the Techichi for Eternity!" proclaimed the Great Hound as his eyes turned white and his coat began to sparkle and glow, and he grew so fast that he quickly covered the whole sky!

The Techichi scattered and tried to hide, but they were too big to conceal themselves anywhere. They all fell sense-less and went into a very deep sleep and dreamed of a new world.

When they awoke, they noticed that they had more

room. The ends of the Earth were now much further away. They could fit between the trees. And there was so much game that they knew they would never run out.

Wowwow spoke to the Techichi: "The Great Hound has enlarged Aztlan! A thousand times! Maybe a million! We shall eat as much as we want forever! We shall never fill this land to overflowing with our poopies! It is ours forever! And still we have our great hearts and our great spirits! We will always be the Techichi!"

And they all pranced away to explore this new, larger Aztlan.

The Great Hound of the Cosmos, his job done, went about his business, and it was many much time periods later that he heard that the Techichi believed that the universe had been expanded just to accommodate them.

The Great Hound laughed. "That does not surprise me! It wasn't my intention to fool them. They are great of heart and great of spirit. That is enough."

The great gods also had moved on, repairing Mu-Dule-Zik-Zok and going to the theater and watching soccer and attending garden parties. One day, someone asked Kev-M-Mikta what had happened with the Techichi.

"I don't know," she admitted. "I had entirely forgotten about the whole affair. I guess it worked itself out."

THE WAR WITH SHOVEL-MOUTH

Know ye, O Children of Ouaca the Terrible, who created all things from her rotting teeth, that there was a time when the Techichi rejected the wise counsel of Aruxa their Queen and waged war with Tamamamun the Shovel-Mouth.

"Why do we only eat small things and dead things? Like lizards and insects and dead lizards and dead tiny horses?"

"I want to play with the lizards. They are nice."

"And we should be riding the tiny horses, not eating the dead ones."

"You can't ride the dead ones, dummy!"

Wowwow the rebel cautioned them against saying dumb things to the air where Ouaca might hear them and get angry and tear them to pieces with her mighty reeking gums.

Then Wowwow forgot his point and they all ran off to bark at some crows who weren't doing anything.

Then it was time for a nap with one Techichi on watch to wake them if Mool the Spotted Tiger or Clemaz the Coyote or Wolf the Wolf wandered too close.

When Wowwow awoke, he remembered what he was saying and continued.

"We Techichi are giant folk! With great souls and giant hearts! Our footprints are like the sea and our legs are tree trunks!"

"True! True!"

"So why do we eat insects and dead things and little birds?"

"And peanuts!"

"No, we like the peanuts! We'll keep eating the peanuts!"

"But no more dead birds and baby mice and stale tortilla chips!"

"But what shall we eat then, O great and wise and bossy rebel chief?"

Wowwow grinned. It was his moment of triumph! He would soon wrest leadership of the Techichi from the Old Lady Queen Aruxa, with her white whiskers and her cataracts and her silly tongue sticking out.

"Tonight, we shall feast on Shovel-Mouth!"

They still had sick smiles on their faces, but Wowwow's little outlaw band didn't seem too enthusiastic. They looked at each other uncomfortably.

Shovel-Mouth was the largest land mammal alive at

time, almost twice as big as the modern-day African elephant. Shovel-Mouth roamed the wet parts of Aztlan, frequenting streams and swamps and ponds in herds of 10 to 20 animals, gathering vegetable matter from the riverbeds with their big stupid shovel mouths.

"Shovel-Mouth is kinda big, Wowwow."

"Are we not the Techichi?! Are we not the giants in this land?!"

"Well, yes, but ..."

"But what?"

"Well, we're not as giant as Shovel-Mouth!"

"Yeah, we're the sensible size of giant!"

"You said it! Shovel-Mouth is ridiculous!"

"He's ridiculously big! He's so big he's silly!"

"And we should eat Shovel-Mouth!"

Wowwow seemed pretty confident, so the rebel band shrugged their shoulders and agreed to support Wowwow in his campaign against Tamamamun.

However, as they'd recently feasted on a half a bag of potato chips and most of an order of chili fries in the gutter, Wowwow's rebel pack decided to wait until the next day to begin their savage conspiracy against ridiculously big and clearly edible Shovel-Mouth.

That night, the entire Techichi pack got together in the Canyon of the Moon and everybody gathered around the Old Lady Queen Aruxa to tell what they'd done during the day.

Being entirely lacking in guile or subtlety, Wowwow's rebel pack looked mightily guilty when it was their turn to brag about the day. They mentioned the potato chips and the chili fries and then looked at each other shiftily.

The Old Lady Queen Aruxa sighed and tilted her head and stared at Wowwow and his little pack of rebels.

She thought about letting it go and then waiting patiently for the coming disaster. But she decided to call them out and impress the rest of the pack with her prophetic prowess.

"Wowwow!" she yapped at them. "You are in the midst of some grandiose scheme, I can see it."

The whole pack turned and looked at Wowwow and his rebels.

"No, no, no, Great Queen," said Wowwow.

The Old Lady Queen Aruxa fixed her brown stare and bared her gums at them. The rebels squealed; they had no choice. Aruxa ruled them with an iron, taloned paw.

"We're going to stalk and kill and eat Shovel-Mouth!"

The Old Lady Queen Aruxa paused and scratched her cheek with a hind leg.

"Well, I'll not condone it," she said. "However, we are the Techichi! We are giants!"

"But not so ridiculously giant as Shovel-Mouth!" added one of her courtiers.

"Oh no! Not so ridiculously giant as that! It's absurd!" the Queen agreed. "But we ARE giants! And we don't need to prove ourselves by bullying our fellow giants, like Tamamamun the Shovel-Mouth, no matter how ridiculous they are!"

There was much clamor in the crowd as the Techichi affirmed their confident giantness. Finally Queen Aruxa finished chewing on her paw and lifted it for quiet.

"However," she said, "Wowwow and his pack have expressed interest in this endeavor and perhaps it is a worthy enterprise for the Techichi. So I shall not say you can't go. Be blessed by the Great Ouaca and her rotting teeth!"

"May you be blessed by the Great Ouaca and her rotting teeth!" repeated the pack.

So Wowwow and his pack of rebels enjoyed the adulation and praise of the Techichi for several days but didn't actually attract any more recruits for the assault on Shovel-Mouth. But then, it was clear that Wowwow's band numbered enough giants of the Techichi to take down Shovel-Mouth. He wasn't so ridiculously giant as all that!

Finally, after waiting for the rain to stop so they wouldn't get colds, they prepared for the hunt by snacking on peanuts and barking at some mysterious inter-dimensional ghostly entity that some people said was just the mailman.

Some people can be hateful.

Tamamamun the Shovel-Mouth wasn't very far away. He shoveled up vegetable matter from a nearby swamp that was fed by the stream where the Techichi got their water. Wowwow and his rebels crept up to the edge of the swamp on their giant but dainty paws.

"Now!" whispered Wowwow at the top of his giant voice.

And so they stampeded down the bank and then waded into the muddy swamp and yipped and yapped at Shovel-Mouth, who wasn't sure what was going on for a minute.

"He's so ridiculously giant, he doesn't even know we're here!" Wowwow said. "A complete surprise attack!"

Shovel-Mouth had fallen asleep, as Shovel-Mouth is known to do after spending all morning eating leaves and branches and twigs. But no one could sleep through that ruckus!

"What is going on?" he asked, still a bit befuddled. He squinted in the afternoon sun. He heard the yapping and the splashing around, and he was vaguely aware that several tiny entities were biting at his ankles and toes.

"We got him on the run!" Wowwow said.

Shovel-Mouth rolled his eyes. "Uh! The Techichi again! What is it with you guys?"

It wasn't the first time something like this had happened. Several generations of Techichi had passed. But Shovel-Mouth remembered. He was a bit weary of this foolishness in his old age.

So Shovel-Mouth bent down and started trying to butt Wowwow and the rebel pack with his forehead.

"He's just about done!" Wowwow shouted! "Shovel-Mouth for dinner!"

"Shovel-Mouth for dinner!" The pack took up the cry.

Wowwow managed to get a grip on Shovel-Mouth's nose. For in those days, Shovel-Mouth had a very broad nose that was only a few inches long, and it wasn't protected by the thick, leathery skin that covered much of the rest of his body.

"Ouch!" said Shovel-Mouth.

The rest of the rebel pack sensed victory at hand after Shovel-Mouth revealed his weakness by his exclamation. So they began leaping on Shovel-Mouth's face and digging their teeth into his nose.

There was no yapping now. Techichi growling and Shovel-Mouth huffing and puffing, yes. And also cursing and telling them to get their stinky Techichi carcasses off his face.

But they were Techichi! They held fast, for they were giants of the land! (Though not quite so giant as Shovel-Mouth, whose giantness was just ridiculous!)

Tamamamun the Shovel-Mouth shook his head violently, and tried to knock them off his face with his big, round feet, but Shovel-Mouth is not that flexible to reach his face with his feet because his massive giantness is absurd.

The Techichi held on, and Shovel-Mouth's nose stretched and stretched, from the size of a grapefruit to the length of a snow deer and finally all the way to the ground.

Wowwow realized that he and his rebel pack were now almost touching the ground at the end of Shovel-Mouth's stretched nose and he could now reach them with his feet. Perhaps Shovel-Mouth was angry enough to smash them flat.

Wowwow let go. "Scatter, my rebels," he said. "We have accomplished our mission and discovered that Shovel-Mouth is not good to eat!"

So the rebel pack all let go and ran in many different directions to safety, with only a few cuts and bruises.

And that, O Children of Ouaca, is how the Techichi discovered that Tamamamun is not good to eat.

And that also is how Tamamamun the Shovel-Mouth got a long trunk instead of a broad nose.

44

WOWWOW'S VISION

O Most Beloved Children of Ouaca the Terrible, she of the Shrill Yapping, the Indomitable Terror of Skateboarders and Bicyclists, gather ye around the garbage bag of loathsome treats and tend to my words and I will tell thee the story of why the Techichi would condescend to live with the pathetic two-legged folk who call themselves the humans.

It was many generations after the war with Shovel-Mouth. And the humans had wandered into the land. They brought fire and they brought tools, which they used with their stupid hands. And they turned away from their nakedness and wore the skins of their prey instead of just eating it and barfing it up later. And also they had something called art which they took out of their heads and channeled into their hands and they used charcoal and blood and chalk and ochre and made pictures of what they dreamed and what they saw. And it was OK, I suppose, but it wasn't that great. But they thought it was really something!

And, lo, the humans set about wiping out the large

creatures, like Shovel-Mouth, for they were just too ridiculously big. Absurdly big. It made no sense to be that big. Dummies.

And among the Techichi, there lived one named Wowwow. He was descended from the Wowwow who had led the Techichi to the city of the great gods, and also from the Wowwow who had led the rebel Techichi in the war against Shovel-Mouth, and he was just as brave and just as rebellious and just as full of himself and just as stubborn as his ancestors.

Wowwow and his band of rebels were pursuing a wounded Longhorn who had been hurt in a mating battle with another Longhorn. He had wandered away to be by himself, and perhaps to recover enough to survive an encounter with a predator, like the wolf or the coyote or the big cat.

Or the Mighty Techichi!

The Techichi found him. The Longhorn kept going, always aware of the Techichi. When they came too close, he clattered around to smash them under hoof and he lowered his head at them so they could see his horns, and thus he warned them that death awaited those who took his minor wounds to be much worse than they were.

"It's just a matter of time, butt-breath," taunted Wow-wow. "You'll get tired and that'll be it. And we'll strip your bones clean, stupid."

The Longhorn sighed. "I'm not hurt that bad, dumb Techichi."

"Oh, whatever," said Wowwow. "You'll die in a minute. Maybe two minutes, Smelly Beast."

"I walked ten miles before you saw me," the Longhorn said. "I'm not gonna just fall down now."

"Your face is stupid, your hoofs are cracked, your butt is dehydrated and swollen, your horns are moldy, you got snot all over your face, your eyes are watery and you got mushrooms growing in your pits," Wowwow said. "You've just about had it."

Longhorn snorted. "That stuff's not even true. Who are you trying to convince? Not me. I know better. And could you lay off some of that name-calling? It's unnecessary and excessive. I get it that you're the hunter and I'm the prey, it's the Circle of Life. Blah blah blah. But, SHEESH! Be a professional! If you keep that up, I'll be trying to smash you flat even if I don't have to, just to shut you up!"

"We're getting to him, boys!" said Wowwow. "Fat Thighs can't take much more of this, with his stupid hot-breathed nostrils and his filthy, smelly ears and his greasy, matted fur."

Longhorn rolled his eyes. Not long after, he turned around and stomped all over the Techichi, killing one and encouraging the others to keep their distance. Longhorn could

47

barely hear Wowwow's taunts, though he shouted as loud as he could.

Wowwow was very hoarse and short of breath after a few hours of this.

"We'll get him," Wowwow croaked to his band of Techichi. "Just a few more minutes. He'll be as dead as a doornail in ten seconds."

Longhorn rolled his eyes and strolled to a grove of trees to hide from larger predators. The Techichi kept their distance. "To lull him into a false sense of security," Wowwow whispered as he curled up for a nap.

Longhorn dozed off a little. When he woke up, he crept away because the Techichi had fallen asleep.

Soon, the Techichi were awakened by a ruckus in the distance. They could hear Longhorn moaning and the sounds of footsteps and scuffling. And, most ominous of all, the shouts of the Tolta, the two-legged folk who called themselves "man."

"Oh, no!" shouted Wowwow. "After we did all the hard work, the humans showed up at the last minute and finished him off!"

"Dumb humans!"

"Stupid Tolta!"

"With their silly opposable thumbs and their Satanic higher reasoning abilities and their way-too-high two-leggedness!"

"They think they're so hot!"

"They look like they were designed by aliens!"

Everyone had a good laugh over that, but they quickly scampered over the hill to see what could be salvaged from the carcass of Longhorn after the meddling of the humans.

And all trotting over the hill and jumping over rocks

and almost bumping into each other … they were adorable.

The Tolta had seen the Longhorn and stayed out of sight as they tracked him into a canyon. Then they attacked him from the sides where he had trouble getting at them, spearing him and dropping rocks on him until the great hunter Nimurz felt confident to rush up and deliver the killing blow with a spear thrust to the heart.

The Techichi were quite shocked.

"Well, that wasn't very sporting!"

"The humans cheat! They use sharp sticks!"

"And their ridiculous reasoning abilities! I mean, it's like second-dimensional chess! Who does that?"

"Not fair! Not fair!"

"You don't suppose … ALIENS taught them how to do that?" implied Wowwow.

They all had a good laugh and waited for the Tolta to cut away the meat they needed and then leave the remains in the sun. The Techichi rushed in and cleaned the bones. It was actually a pretty good dinner for a small group of Techichi.

Wowwow began thinking about that. The Techichi were big and fierce, the biggest and fiercest of creatures! They didn't need to be as big as Shovel-Mouth. (He was ridiculously big!) They didn't need to cheat and use tools. Or have highly developed reasoning facilities. (Which is just dumb.) Or have stupid-looking opposable thumbs. Or walk on two legs, which is absurd. You keep expecting them all to lose their balance and fall down at the same time!

Wowwow knew that would happen eventually. When it does, the Techichi will laugh themselves silly.

The Techichi are the greatest folk on Earth, Wowwow knew. So why should they suffer the cheating ways of the stupid Tolta and their cheater tools and their stupid thumbs (so ugly!) and their awkward and graceless two-leggedness and their unsporting higher reasoning facilities?

"NO!" Wowwow said. "It isn't right! Ouaca wouldn't let this happen! She of the rotten teeth that give life to all things! Ouaca, on whose hairless pink belly we all live! The Goddess of the Techichi, she who watches over all her children, and nourishes the life-giving lands with her excretions and whose liquid vomit washes away all the evil that bedevils her children the Techichi! Surely she must see the injustice! Surely she will not let this stand!"

Wowwow said all this out loud, and all the merry rebels of his outlaw Techichi band looked at him admiringly, for they loved speeches and though it might have sounded like annoying, shrill yapping to the humans, the Techichi heard it as though the Great Hound of the Cosmos was speaking directly through Wowwow.

"Ouaca looks out for her children!" Wowwow said. "There must be a reason for our recent humiliation!"

"Duh!" said the nearest Techichi.

"I didn't think it was so humiliating," said another.

"We all had enough to eat."

"We came out of it pretty well."

"Yeah, the dumb humans did all the work with their dumb thumbs and their stupid walking upright thing. What's up with THAT?"

"Yeah, who does that? They look like they're all going to fall over at the first gust of wind."

One of Wowwow's little band blew on them and the Techichi all laughed and fell over on their backs with their legs sticking up, mocking that time in the future they knew would come when all the humans would fall down at the same time.

And so they reclined in the sun until it was time to find some muddy forest ponds to drink from and some stop signs to pee on. The Techichi spent the rest of the day on such pursuits, barking at gardeners, charging coyotes, spitting up grass, chewing on their feet, sniffing the poop of other animals, and just generally frolicking.

But not Wowwow.

He followed them, walking slowly and thinking and pondering the revelations of the day. Sometimes he had to run to catch up with the pack. Once he was distracted for a short time by some particularly interesting poop. And again when they all ate some bugs.

Finally, it hit him. The Techichi didn't eat as much as the Tolta. The humans left plenty of food when they killed a big animal like a Longhorn.

Maybe the Techichi should just follow them around, let

the Tolta do the work, and the Techichi could swoop in at the end and eat their fill of the bounteous remains!

"Hey, Techichi, my faithful pack of the yappy Children of Ouaca!" said Wowwow.

They all looked up from their naps and licking their groins and sniffing pee and eating bugs and barking at the guy delivering water. For this was Wowwow, the Prophet of Ouaca, and he would have something profound to say to them.

"I've been thinking about this day and our bounteous feast," said Wowwow. "We did all the work and the big dumb Tolta humans came in at the last minute and got the credit for the kill."

"Cheaters!"

"Two-legged freaks!"

"Their front and back paws show a frightening variety in shape and appearance!"

"I know, right? Like two different animals!"

They laughed and it went on for a while, but eventually Wowwow got back on track.

"We shouldn't do the work!" he said. "They should do it! Look at us! The Truly Blessed Children of Ouaca! The Great Hound of the Cosmos has blessed us and found us worthy of his notice! The Wolf of the Sun smiles on our endeavors!"

They all thought about The Wolf of the Sun for a minute and felt safe knowing he was their protector.

"So we'll follow the humans around and let them do the work!" Wowwow proclaimed, temporarily gifted with an unusual capacity to stick to the point.

"Oh, yeah!"

"Great idea!"

"The worthless, silly-looking Tolta humans will jump at

the chance to serve us, the Blessed Children of Ouaca!"

"We can help them get back up when they all fall at same time, as we expect will happen any day now!"

"Yes!" Wowwow said. "We must always be ready to jump in and help so they don't suspect that THEY are serving US! We will warn them when the gardeners or the pool guy arrive to do their evil. We will warn of bicyclists and roller skaters when it looks like they are coming too close. We will keep them warm at night. We will be there for them when they are sad. We will pee in the house because it is hilarious and it will make them laugh and they will be happy."

And so the Techichi began their scheme the next day. They sniffed out the Tolta village and found great enjoyment in a ravine nearby where the humans tossed things they no longer needed. This included many items that might be considered garbage by some but looked like food to the Techichi.

"This was a really good idea, Wowwow! You are a great leader!"

The Tolta noticed the activities of the Techichi and reported them to the chief.

"Hey, Taka, Tolta chief. There's some little dogs living in our midden."

"Well, I guess that's OK," said Taka. "Maybe it won't stink so bad if it's being policed by little dogs. Plus their barking will warn us of intruders. You know, like the mailman or a pizza delivery guy."

And so the Techichi moved into the outskirts of Tolta society.

"This isn't so bad," said Wowwow. "We get the food they don't eat. We devour many delicious rats and mice. We're safer. They only occasionally kill one of us for dinner."

"Yeah, we got it good from our two-legged servants!

If their advanced brains are so great, how come they're doing all the work for us?"

Soon the Techichi felt comfortable enough to go with the younger Tolta to hunt rabbits and squirrels and prey like that. It was fun for the Techichi, it was great sport to chase a groundhog or a beaver into a gully and then bark and run around until the young humans ran up to kill it.

"Ain't this the life?" said Wowwow. "Free food. Recreation. Lodging. It's just like a spa."

"Yeah, you're a great leader, Wowwow!"

"And the dumb humans think that we're doing work, like we're babysitters!"

"Dumb humans!"

"It's only a matter of time before a strong wind knocks them down all at the same time!"

They all laughed.

And soon after, the Techichi were living in the caves and the huts with the Tolta. Wowwow moved in with Taka the chief. He woke Taka up in the middle of the night to warn him of ghosts. Wowwow frequently vomited on the floor. Wowwow kept Taka warm at night. The Techichi leader was often underfoot and sometimes Taka worried about stepping on him.

Elah, Taka's wife, was also fond of Wowwow. "He keeps me company when I am hunting and gathering.

"He makes Taka Jr. laugh. I like to dress him up at harvest time."

"He catches rats and mice right around the house instead of just in the midden," said Taka. "He lets us know if someone is sneaking up to the cave entrance. And he barks at evil spirits so we have time to wave our talismans and protect ourselves."

"This is great," Wowwow told his rebel band

which had grown until it had infiltrated every family among the Tolta. "We get food. We have all the Tolta people as our recreation directors and servants. We live in safety in their villages. We have warm beds."

"And they think we're pets!"

"Stupid dumb humans!"

"But they've grown on me. I like it when they pet me with their stupid hands."

"And they are up so high! They can carry me around and I can see everything from way above the ground and I can lick their faces!"

"Yeah! I like them! We're lucky they had the good sense to serve us so they can get the same blessings that Ouaca and the Great Hound of the Cosmos and The Wolf of the Sun also bestow on us, the Fierce and Brave and Terrible Techichi tribe!"

Yes. And everyone agreed that Wowwow was the greatest and smartest leader who had ever lived for thinking of such a sweet arrangement.

Many years have passed, and it is still a sweet arrangement as the Techichi continue to guide their helpless servants, the humans.

And the Techichi are still waiting for that moment they know will come, when the humans will all fall down at the same time because of their awkward, vertical two-leggedness.

After which, the Techichi will roll on their backs and laugh and laugh.

THE WAY OF THE DEAD

Tibu saw the little dog sleeping by the doorway, soaking up the rays of the late morning sun. He shook his head. It was a hot day and it would get hotter. But the silly dog always found a place to sleep where the sun was hottest.

Tibu looked around to make sure no one was around. He wanted to sneak up on the dog and tease her a little. Xenti, usually a playful if aggressive little dog, would snarl and try to bite if bothered while asleep. It made Tibu laugh. But Xenti was a temple dog, the personal guardian of the high priest, and Tibu would be punished if anybody saw him being disrespectful to her.

It was the beginning of the hottest part of the day and the priests had retreated to the inner chambers of the temple. The servants had retired to one of the shady courtyards to nap or to chat or to work on some of the less strenuous chores.

Tibu decided it would be a good time to tease Xenti. Just a little. He walked softly on bare feet and bent down next

to her. He blew on her head. He playfully tugged on her ears.
She didn't respond.

She grunted a little when he scratched her throat. Finally, he grabbed her tummy and shook her lightly.

Now Xenti was awake! She snarled. She growled. She showed her teeth. She tried to bite him but he yanked his hand away.

"Ha ha, Xenti," he whispered. "Did you really mean to bite me?"

Xenti snarled at him again. Tibu sat down cross-legged and put his hands on the stone floor.

Xenti sniffed cautiously, then crawled into his lap as he scratched her throat.

They sat together for a few minutes, then Tibu took Xenti into the temple garden so she could chase after lizards.

Suddenly, Xenti stopped in the middle of a step and stared intently at the black garden wall. The lizards scampered away, unharmed and unnoticed. Tibu stood very still and watched her. Tibu might not be particularly heedful of all the rules of conduct of the temple but he knew enough to leave the temple dogs alone when they looked into the spirit world.

The Techichi spend a lot of time in realms that man cannot see. And they must not be disturbed! They are learning about the unknown lands beyond human perception and the many paths within. Most importantly, the Way of the Dead.

If you are an important person, you take your Techichi with you, and he leads you along the Way of the Dead and directs you to Paradise. So it is important for the Techichi to know the way.

What did Xenti see?

The priests say it is cloudy, and your newly dead eyes will see only vague shapes and shadows. It is easy to lose your way, to go down the wrong path, to find yourself in the various kingdoms of the gods of pain. Zhor, who strips off the flesh of those who disobey the purity laws. Fin-Kun-Ta, who consumes the hands of thieves and saves two fingerbones to shove into your eye sockets. Ka-Vuh the Devourer, who lives off the souls of the faithless ones who would betray their loyal servants and friends.

There are many of these demons. The spirit world overflows with cliffs and waterfalls and thick forests and dry canyons and quicksand and many other hazards that lead to the demons and their hells and their infernos and their torture mansions.

The unwary soul can get lost and wander forever in the Forgotten Desert or the Endless Ocean or the Long Steep Stairwell With No End.

There are many hells, but only one heaven. Its blazing, welcoming light waits behind a great mountain of doom, but once you get around the cliffs to the other side of the great crag, the comforting heat of the sun god Zacatek leads you to his side in Paradise.

"Being a good person" is apparently not good enough. Or maybe it's just too difficult to be a good person. You take an extra dessert when no one is looking. You don't like your co-worker's wife and your reasons aren't very convincing. You stepped on bugs when you couldn't help it. You cut out the heart of a war captive because the god of blood Takakukl demands it for a good harvest or victory in war or earthquake protection. You aren't always scrupulous of all of the rules of the temple. It's hard. It's a lot to remember.

Well, whatever. When you die, you'll need every advantage to even have a chance at heaven. So your dog has to go with you.

Tibu leaned over and braced himself against a wall as slowly as he could and watched Xenti.

The little dog stood motionless with brows furrowed, mouth curled slightly, looking at the beige stone of the garden wall. Xenti put forward her paw on the tile walkway. Eventually, she settled herself on the ground, chest to tile, her paws under her ribs as her eyes never left that indistinct point on the wall.

Finally, she put her head down and, seemingly exhausted, dozed off. Tibu carried her out of the sun and put her in a bed of cloth in one of the temple hallways.

"I wonder what Xenti saw?" Tibu mused to himself. "It must have been very important! The high priest will get to heaven very quickly when the time comes."

Knowing that the kitchen staff would be getting back to work after the siesta, Tibu hurried back to his station. Helping to look after the temple dogs wasn't the only daily task he was responsible for. He might be sent to get water. He might cut the kernels off the maize. He might grind taro or manioc or yams or something like that.

Today, he would be harvesting chia seeds! Well, it wasn't the worst way to spend the late afternoon.

A few hours later, after Tibu had eaten his late meal of tortillas, maize and beans, he sought out Xenti and took her to play in the garden with the other temple dogs.

Xenti wasn't that old, but she could be very grumpy and irritable with the younger dogs. She usually got over it pretty quickly as soon as they were all done sniffing, and soon they were all chasing each other around the garden and barking at birds.

Tibu leaned against the garden wall and watched the dogs. He smiled. Xenti clearly ruled the pack, but they all had their personalities, their disputes and their interests.

He dozed off for a few minutes. Tibu had skipped siesta time and his weariness caught up with him. He awoke to find Jin-Jin standing close by and snorting at him. She rolled over on her back and he scratched her tummy.

Xenti saw this and rushed over jealously. She was very attached to Tibu and temporarily resented this brazen interloper. Xenti and Jin-Jin rolled around for a few seconds, snapping at each other and growling, until Tibu picked them up and placed them on opposite sides of his torso.

He smiled again and dozed off, to be awakened a few minutes later because Patxi had wandered over and started a fight with Xenti in Tibu's lap.

These dogs.

Some weeks later, the high priest stumbled in a corridor. The retainers carried him to his chambers and sent for the medicine man. The high priest woke up, but he was very weak. At times, he could scarcely take a breath.

After a few weeks with no improvement, everyone in the temple knew that the end was near for the high priest. The council chose a successor. And the temple dog Xenti was set aside for ritual purification before the death ceremony.

Tibu's father sent him away for a few days. He feared Tibu would embarrass the family with an emotional outburst when he realized what would happen to Xenti. But it was the way of the temple dog. Xenti was the high priest's protector. Xenti was the holy wayfarer. It would not be right to defy the gods and take a risk that the high priest might get lost and end up in one of the nasty hells in the spirit world.

The high priest passed away in his sleep. Xenti passed away not so peacefully, knocked unconscious with a rock and then quickly dispatched with a ceremonial knife.

Tibu lived only a few more years, barely making it to the cusp of manhood when he was killed in battle when his city attacked another city because reasons.

The spirit world was cloudy and almost colorless. Tibu felt like he could reach out and touch the bland, sepia sky. He didn't care much who had won the battle. He scarcely realized that he was dead now, facing the perils of the spirit world.

At the first fork in the scraggly path, he halted, still a bit dazed. It dawned on him that he must be in the spirit world. One moment he had been holding a spear and gritting his teeth. And now, he was here. Was it a dream?

He was pretty sure it wasn't a dream.

Tibu heard some faraway yapping. Still fighting off a little brain fatigue, he looked into the distance, his vision limited by the gray fog. The high-pitched yapping seemed to be getting closer.

The shroud around his mind dissipated as he finally recognized the dog's bark. It was Xenti!

Yes, he had died and the spirit world surrounded him. And Xenti soon would greet him and lead him to Paradise.

Xenti's barking seemed to come from every direction, so he waited at the fork in the trail. How much time passed he did not know. It didn't seem very long.

Xenti appeared from the mist and wagged her tail and danced on her hind legs, for she was so happy to see Tibu. He laughed and picked her up and buried his face in her belly and then held her close so she could lick his face and ears.

"It is good to see you, Xenti," he said. "I feel safe now. And content."

He hugged her a few moments more, but Xenti became restless and began struggling to get free.

Tibu released her and she ran two circles around him, and then ran down the right fork a few steps, then turned and barked at him.

"Of course, Xenti," he said. "It is the spirit world and it is dangerous to dawdle. Guide me through the way of the dead, and we will have a lot of time to catch up in Paradise."

Xenti barked excitedly and trotted along the trail, urging Tibu to hurry.

Tibu followed, completely trusting his little guide to the afterlife. Soon he felt so comfortable that he began speaking about their time together in the temple. Chasing the brightly-colored birds. Jin-Jin and Patxi and the other temple dogs. Old Mara the head cook and her secret recipe for sweet cornbread. And Sun Face, the old monkey that lived in a corner of the garden.

And the high priest.

"I should be surprised to see you, I think," Tibu said. "Weren't you supposed to guide the high priest to Paradise? I didn't know you could go to Paradise and then come back and guide someone else."

Xenti stopped and looked over her shoulder at him. Then she turned and ran at him, and then in circles, barking and prancing around in front of him. Then she stopped and glared at him.

Tibu, startled, stopped and examined her closely. Xenti's brows tightened at the bridge of her snout. Her eyes glistened with anger. It took Tibu a few moments to realize that Xenti understood what he was saying ... and she didn't like it!

"You ... you understand me?"

Xenti barked once and nodded in agreement.

"Have you been to Paradise?"

Xenti jumped up and down, barking. Then she looked into his face and shook her head to tell him: no.

"You waited for me?" he asked, a few tears in his eyes.

Xenti barked once and nodded.

"Well, what happened to the high priest?"

Xenti looked around slowly, prompting Tibu to examine his surroundings. The mist had darkened. Black, menacing spots like those of a jaguar floated in the distance. They seemed to be getting larger.

"Did something bad happen to the high priest?"

Xenti looked into his face, barked and nodded.

"What happened to him?"

Xenti looked into the spreading darkness, then looked back at Tibu. She jumped off the trail and ran into the mist, barking loudly so he could follow.

Tibu hurried after her. He could see he didn't have much time. Maybe this little detour wasn't such a good idea, but Xenti had committed herself to leading him off the trail to Paradise to see … something.

Waves of heat pounded at him, and he could see flashes of black lightning in the distance. His head began to ache. He realized his nose had started bleeding.

Xenti, barking loudly, jumped on his knees and stopped him from tumbling into the abyss.

Tibu started to sit down but Xenti bit his ankles and his butt to get him to stand up straight. Then Xenti perched on the edge of the chasm and barked loudly and persistently.

"It's fine, Xenti!" Tibu shouted over the racket the little dog was making. "I don't need to know what happened to the high priest!"

"Oh, it's too late for that, good little soul!" said a booming voice, accompanied by the hot breath of hell, .

smelling like a ton of rotten tomatoes and a dozen old deer carcasses.

The image started shimmering in the darkness of the crevasse, two faces, one purple and one yellow. The purple visage appeared fair and serene and even healthy. The yellow face, angry and fearful, exhibited signs of decay, bloody patches, torn skin, a nose mostly eaten away by misfortune and disease, sad eyes, a few black teeth, a crooked jaw.

"Ka-Vuh!" said Tibu, almost soundlessly.

"Don't speak again, good little soul," said Ka-Vuh. "If my reputation precedes me, you should know not to speak in my presence. You are a good soul and you don't belong to me. But it is not unknown for me to take that which isn't mine!"

The giant faces of Ka-Vuh grew until they seemed to stretch from one horizon to the next. As if he had leaned closer to examine this intruder and his little dog.

Then they receded a little.

Xenti growled. A very low growl. But very persistent.

"You have little to fear from me, good little soul," said Ka-Vuh. "You have the love and protection of this great spirit beside you. I have great respect for the Techichi. This audacious creature brought you to my pit of despair just because you asked!

"She did not lead the high priest to Paradise because it was never her choice to do so! He was mine! He was mine from the moment that he agreed that his loyal companion would be killed when he died so she could lead him to Paradise.

"For I am the god who punishes the disloyal, those who would betray their friends and servants, and this was a great betrayal."

Ka-Vuh laughed.

"My pit is full of men and women like your high priest

66

who put ritual and habit ahead of common kindness. The years will pass, the world will change. I will never lack for new subjects."

He laughed again.

"Now go, good little soul. Or you will never get to Paradise."

The faces of Ka-Vuh disappeared. Tibu, still a bit stunned by the experience, had to concentrate to hear Xenti barking behind him. He turned and hurried towards Xenti's frantic exhortations.

It was pitch black all around him. The skies grew even darker when the black lightning flashed. He followed Xenti's yaps until he reached the trail.

Xenti barked frantically and ran circles around him, then darted along the path, the only visible light glowing faintly from her footprints.

Tibu felt confident that, with Xenti's guidance, he would make it safely to Paradise.

THE LITTLE DOG WITH THE MUDDY FEET
WHO SAVED THE WEST

1.

The inspiration for this story began with a couple of sentences in a book about the history of the exploration, the colonization and the development of commercial trade routes in the American Southwest and northern Mexico. The image in my head of this little incident showed some promise, but it wasn't that easy to turn it into a short story. I just kept asking myself: What else does it need? And when I devised an answer, I then had to engineer a way to express it in prose.

It wasn't my intention to write a story that teaches history. It was an accident. It just didn't seem like a story without some context, and that context turned it into historical fiction.

I hope there are at least a few readers out there who find some value in it.

2.

Excerpt from "Great Assholes of History"

Juan de Oñate y Salazar (1550 to 1626)

Madre de dios! Este pendejo! I can't even with this guy!

He's most famous for his time as Spain's colonial governor of the province of Santa Fe. In 1599, he ordered the soldiers under his command to massacre the native people at the Acoma pueblo, 60 miles west of the present site of Albuquerque. An estimated 800 to 1,000 men, women and children were murdered. Another thousand were enslaved. Twenty-four had a hand or a foot amputated.

And what did the Acoma people do to deserve this fate?

Several weeks before the mass murder event, Oñate's nephew Juan de Zaldívar went to the pueblo with 16 men and demanded food and shelter. The Acoma people had heard of the colonial government's plan to relocate the inhabitants of the pueblo to a new location where they would be forced to convert to Christianity and to work for the crown. So the Acoma refused to cooperate with the Spanish raiders.

Zaldívar and his men entered some homes in the pueblo, stealing food and blankets, and the Acoma people, who had been trading peacefully with the Spanish for several months, decided that enough was enough and resisted the pilfering Spaniards, killing Zaldívar and most of his men.

Oñate, who could have reconsidered his Acoma policy at this point, decided that the people of the Acoma pueblo should be punished for defending themselves against pirates. So the Spaniards attacked and murdered about 20% of the population, enslaved another large portion and scattered about half of the population and torched the pueblo.

So. Yeah. What an asshole.

Oñate was born in 1550 in Zacatecas, the son of a conquistador who had stayed in Mexico and made a fortune mining silver. Oñate's ancestry included the House of Haro and, on his mother's side, many conversos, former Jews who had converted to Christianity in the 1300s for fear of being murdered after a wave of anti-Semitic violence left tens of thousands of Spanish Jews dead.

In 1588, Oñate married Isabel de Tolosa Cortés de Montezuma, who was not only the granddaughter of Hernan Cortés but was also the great-granddaughter of Moctezuma II.

Oñate also established the Chihuahua Trail, from the town of Chihuahua through the desert of what is now northern Mexico, to cross the Rio Grande near modern-day Juarez, and then north to Santa Fe. The Chihuahua Trail expanded Spanish control further north, opening the way for further expansion into what is now Texas, New Mexico, Arizona and southern California. In later centuries, traders and explorers from the United States would travel the Santa Fe Trail from Missouri to hook up with the northern end of the Chihuahua Trail, and it became part of the trading network of the Southwest.

3.

Excerpt From "The Book of Trails"

The Chihuahua Trail

The Chihuahua Trail connected what is now the southwestern territories of the United States with Spain's American empire and (after the 1820s) with Mexico.

Starting just north of the present-day city of Chihuahua, the Chihuahua Trail led almost straight north, veering to the northeast or northwest based on the terrain and the availability of water.

The distance from Chihuahua to the present-day location of El Paso is more than 200 miles. The trail continued north to Santa Fe for another 300 miles. The Rio Grande turns northerly as it passes into present-day New Mexico, and the Chihuahua Trail followed it for much of the remaining distance to Santa Fe.

However, there was a 90-mile stretch where the banks of the river were too treacherous for wagons, so the trail abandoned the river and crossed into the desert. This nearly waterless section of the trail was called "El Jornado del Muerto," the March of Death.

The Chihuahua Trail connected Spain's empire in what is now northern Mexico with Santa Fe, which eventually became the eastern end of a thoroughfare with the Spanish colonies in California via a tentative pathway through modern-day New Mexico and Arizona which became known as the Old Spanish Trail.

As the territories of the United States moved west, the Chihuahua Trail was one of several pathways of trade with one end in Santa Fe. The other two were the Santa Fe Trail (connecting Santa Fe with St. Louis, Missouri) and the Old Spanish Trail (connecting Santa Fe with Los Angeles), thus establishing contact between Mexico, California and the United States through a trade network in the early 1800s.

4.

Excerpt from Oñate's journal

May 20, 1598 - We were unable to follow the river past

the Cerro de Rojo. The banks are steep and barren. Nothing but cactus and dried brush. This is a mean, sterile, merciless country. I hate it so much I could POOP!

Unless you like Gila monsters and tarantulas and rattle-snakes and thorn trees. If that's your thing, knock yourself out! Even the turtles are poisonous!

Fortunately, the native people are deprived, half-starved and easy to kill and intimidate. Our European diseases have preceded us and laid waste to the countryside, cutting down these degenerates like wheat at harvest time. Ha ha!

I took some of the food-bags with me to go ahead of the caravan to look for water. I'm sure at least one of us will make it back.

May 21, 1598 - We had breakfast at a disreputable-looking taco stand. It was either that or Arby's.

It didn't look too promising in any direction. I split the advance party into two groups. I led my group to the north-west and I put one of the food-bags in charge of a party going to the northeast. Juan is not a bad fellow. I probably should not have sent Robledo in his group, but I have had my fill of Robledo. It would be bad for morale if the men saw me stran-gle Robledo with my bare hands and I don't want to increase the beatings or decrease the rations again.

May 22, 1598 – We walked around for a while and did-n't see any water. So after a time we went back to the taco stand to get some sodas. The Galicians insist on calling it pop so I had them whipped.

May 23, 1598 – The other group found water! Appar-ently, they saw a little dog with muddy feet and followed it to water. I asked Juan why they didn't kill it and eat it. Good protein. He said that it would have been very ungrateful to kill the creature that had very likely saved the whole expedition.

He's not going to go very far in the Spanish army. I may transfer him back to the expedition to be a wet-nurse.

That is the good news.

The other good news is the report that Robledo was killed and buried in the desert. I asked how he died and Juan told me Robledo fell off a cliff. He seemed a little unnerved in telling me this. They are kinsman, so I suspect that Robledo was horsing around and probably fell while acting out some witless japes or perhaps bananashenanigans.

5.

LETTERS

From Juan Almodovar Lopes y Garrilla to Josefia Maria Yrigoyen y Yribarren

May 21, 1599

It is with a heavy heart that I must tell you of the death of our friend Pedro Robledo. After all we've been through since leaving Chihuahua, it seems a cruel prank of fate to say sayonara to Pedro el payaso!

And yet, it is hard to say he did not, in part, bring it on himself. It is a strange country we are traveling through. Barren, treacherous, cruel. Some might call it enchanted, but any magic here is black magic. It might be better to say "cursed" instead of "enchanted."

One should tread carefully, very carefully indeed.

But you know Pedro! He wasn't called el payaso for nothing!

We kept seeing bones, various animal bones. Rodents, cattle, dogs. And sometimes human bones.

I imagine that Pedro had been cooking up some ideas

for a prank for days. Finally, he picked up a human skull and began to interrogate it.

"Hey, Esqueletito! How are you?"

And then he turned the face of the skull towards us and answered as if he were the skull. "Not so good, señor. My wife, you know, she's not such a great cook."

Pedro laughed. The rest of us looked on, horrified. There were two native guides with us, two sturdy fellows from the Mansos people. They were more than horrified.

Pedro continued. "That's too bad, Esqueletito. Hey! Do you know where the next water hole is?"

The skull answered back, "I was wondering that myself. I'm pretty sure you'll never find it, pendejo.

"I wish I could help! NOT!"

Pedro thought this very amusing and laughed uproariously.

The Mansos guides threw themselves on the ground, shrieking in their savage tongue, presumably asking for forgiveness from their ancestors for accidentally witnessing Pedro's performance.

The rest of us stood there a bit dazed, unsure of what to do. One by one, we began clutching our rosaries and asking for mercy from any local spirits who might be displeased by Pedro's impromptu blasphemy.

Pedro, realizing that his little jest had proven to be too sophisticated for his audience, put down the skull. He looked at the native guides, groveling and convulsing in the dirt, and turned white. He clutched at the crucifix around his neck and muttered a few words in the general direction of the sun. Then he shrugged his shoulders and started off across the desert.

We were supposed to be looking for water.

We followed, still shaken and nervous. The Mansos

guides caught up to us about thirty minutes later, still looking scared and maybe a bit apprehensive.

It had been a foolish impulse to mock the dead in this unfriendly land. Pedro didn't get a chance to make amends, even if such a thing were possible.

An hour or so passed. Pedro had veered off to high ground to look for signs of water, low ground, vegetation that wasn't cactus, animal tracks, anything. ANYTHING!

It was very hot for May. The wind was blowing the dirt around, creating small, circular columns of twirling dust.

Pedro's mood had improved and he was again acting festive and happy and gay. Standing on the ridge with his fists at his waist, he looked out at the arid valley as if he owned it.

"Look! Dust devils!" he said. "As children back in Almería, we chased them for good luck!"

The Mansos guides had caught up with us. They held back, preferring to stay behind the ridge. The interpreter told us that the local people fear these windblown, swirling entities, believing them to be evil spirits risen from the earth and trying to form new bodies. First they use dirt and leaves and brush, but they hope to eventually make use of animals or people.

Pedro laughed. "Ridiculous." He marched into the valley, laughing.

The guides jumped down on the ground and peered over the ridge to see what would happen. We joined them.

We had seen enough of this land to treat it and all its manifestations with caution and respect.

We quickly realized that the dust devil towered over Pedro. The perspective of the sloping ground had provided a deceptive view of the twister's actual size. I had thought the dust devil was three or four feet in height, and I assume Pedro

thought the same.

But the wind shifted, and the devil revealed its true size as it swiftly raced at Pedro, as if by its own will and malice.

I wasn't close enough to see Pedro's expression. I imagine it surprised him to see this force, this deceptive entity of wind and dust and evil, turn out to be, not a trivial child-sized diversion, but a truly dangerous force of 15 feet in height. Nay, not 15, 20 perhaps. Thirty maybe?

He ran and fell and, perhaps confused, pulled himself up and ran in the wrong direction.

And then the spirit (for who could now doubt that it was a malicious spirit?) lifted Pedro into the air. And for a matter of seconds, he was merely a passenger.

The crown of the spirit swiveled about even as poor Pedro circled around in its airy maw. Its rotating motion was very swift and hard to gauge but I'm sure it was four or five times a second at least.

I think Pedro was mercifully dead or unconscious before it threw him to the ground the first time.

The evil force kept slamming Pedro against the sun-baked earth, four times, five times, perhaps six total.

Blood and pieces of his body spread out over a half a mile.

And then it headed off to the north and disappeared into the distance. We voted to tell the commandant that he had fallen off a cliff.

From Juan Almodovar Lopes y Garrilla to Josefina Maria Yrigoyen y Yribarren

May 23, 1599

Jornada del Muerto! This country has tried to kill us like it killed poor Pedro, but we have survived another day, by the grace of God, and also by respecting the demons of this hell. The entrance to Hell, I feel it is close by, perhaps just out of sight to the East, so we have been praying to the Virgin when facing West, and then turning East and appeasing the demons with flattery, with the guidance of the Mansos people. We are not disturbing the bones and we are not mocking this land's demons.

It is sad that Pedro was so disrespectful. He brought it on himself and we are lucky we were not doomed with him.

We saw no sign of water for nearly two days after that. We had nearly given up. We weren't sure we could get back to the wagons to tell them we had failed. We feared we would die on the March of Death and none would ever know our fate.

But Alvarez said he had seen something, an animal perhaps, and we went ahead, to the hill where the creature had been sighted.

I think most of us though it was a mirage, and that Alvarez had seen a fairy brought on by fever and thirst. But we saw it also, and it was now close enough to see that it was a small dog, about 12 pounds, with very short, fine hair, long, thin legs and a head like a deer.

He perched on his haunches and wagged his tail as he waited for us.

"Look! Look at his muddy feet!" Alvarez cried.

It was true. The little dog barked and jumped at our knees as we got close and got his muddy feet all over what was left of our boots and trousers.

He barked and barked and ran in circles until we followed him along the foot of the hill to a mudhole, a low place that was hidden from the sun most of the day by the hill above. In the middle was a patch of standing water, and we could see the dog's footprints leading to and from the cloudy pool.

We filled our canteens and soaked our bandanas and immersed our faces.

That little dog had saved our expedition. The Great and Glorious Empire of Spain would expand further to the north, and we would soon bring Christianity and Spanish civilization to thousands more of these heathen savages.

Glory to Spain and King Philip!

6.

The Little Dog with the Muddy Feet

The little dog, after leading the advance party to water, discreetly excused himself while the soldiers were refreshing themselves. He had heard enough stories about European explorers to know that these desperate adventurers might be hungry enough to eat him despite the fact that he had saved their lives and their expedition. He pranced along beside the hill until he disappeared into a shallow, narrow canyon.

The pack trotted out to meet him.

"Where did you go, Wowwow?"

I went to get some water at the mudhole and I saw some humans coming," said Wowwow.

"Ugh."

"With their dumb vertical two-leggedness!"

"They are going to fall down any day now!"

"I know," said Wowwow. "But these were different. They had solid coverings colored gray and their dumb pink faces were sticking out at the top."

"Well, that's just dumb!"

"What did you do?"

"They were looking very thirsty," said Wowwow.

"I thought they might need water. So I led them to the

waterhole."

"Oh, Wowwow. Now they'll come in great numbers and take all the water and probably kill and eat us. Why did you help them?"

"I thought they might have treats," said Wowwow.

They all agreed that was a good reason.

7.

So that is my story.

Quite a bit of it based on incidents described in historical documents. Oñate was a real person and he was as bad as I've described him. The Acoma massacre was a real event and my version is not far off from the reality of the atrocity. Even Robledo is a real person whose death is mentioned in the records even though my version of events is completely made up because the bare mention of his demise is recorded without any details.

The dog that led them to water and probably saved the expedition may not be real but the incident is briefly described in the records. That tiny segment of the narrative is what inspired the story. I found it very compelling, this brief mention of a small dog with dirty feet who led the soldiers to water.

As I struggled to develop the story, I found I had to keep adding more and more to the odd little tale of the little dog with the muddy feet, providing some historical context for why they were in the desert and what they were doing and the grand plan for Spanish exploitation of the Americas.

I would like to thank the reader for sticking with it to the end of the tale and being patient with my literary experimentation with history, fiction and Chihuahua dogs. I probably won't do it again without a little encouragement.

Tony Seybert was born in Muncie, Indiana, in 1964 and spent the first 24 years of his life in Middletown, Anderson, New Castle and Muncie in the Hoosier state. He moved to Southern California in 1988 and has lived in Hollywood, Lancaster, Palmdale and Chino Hills.

Tony has been a student, a reporter, a copy editor, a cartoonist and various other occupations. He has a master's degree in history from California State University Northridge. His graduate research turned into a thesis on Mississippi journalism to the end of the Civil War.

Tony currently works in pet rescue and lives in San Dimas with various cats and small dogs.